# SOLAR SYSTEM

By S.L. Hamilton

# VISIT US AT
# WWW.ABDOPUBLISHING.COM

Published by ABDO Publishing Company, 8000 West 78th Street, Suite 310, Edina, MN 55439. Copyright ©2011 by Abdo Consulting Group, Inc. International copyrights reserved in all countries. No part of this book may be reproduced in any form without written permission from the publisher. A&D Xtreme™ is a trademark and logo of ABDO Publishing Company.

Printed in the United States of America, North Mankato, Minnesota.
112010
012011

PRINTED ON RECYCLED PAPER

Editor: John Hamilton
Graphic Design: Sue Hamilton
Cover Design:  John Hamilton
Cover Photo: NASA
Interior Photos: All photos by NASA, except page 12 Barringer Meteor Crater, Corbis.

Library of Congress Cataloging-in-Publication Data

Hamilton, Sue L., 1959-
   Solar system / S.L. Hamilton.
     p. cm.
   ISBN 978-1-61714-740-1
   1. Solar system--Juvenile literature. I. Title.
   QB501.3.H36 2011
   523.2--dc22

                          2010041184

# CONTENTS

# XTREME

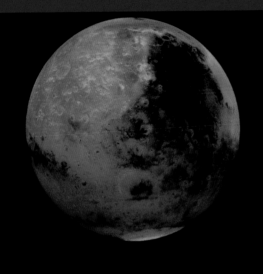

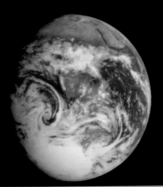

Xtreme Fact

Except for Earth, the planets were named after Greek and Roman gods and goddesses.

# SOLAR SYSTEM

Early scientists saw points of light in the night sky that seemed to move among the stars. They called these special lights "planets," which is a Greek word meaning "wanderers."

# THE

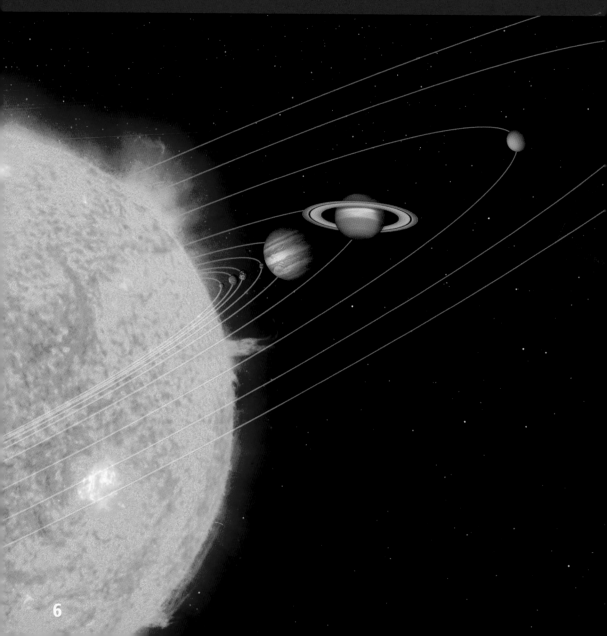

# SUN

The planets in our solar system circle around the Sun. It is 4.6 billion years old. The Sun is a hot ball of glowing gases. Its surface temperature is about 10,000 degrees Fahrenheit (5,538°C).

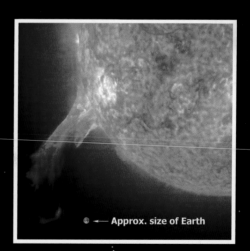

⊕ ◄— Approx. size of Earth

**Xtreme Fact**

The Sun is huge. About 1.3 million Earths would fit in the Sun.

# PLANET

Mercury is the smallest planet. It is also closest to the Sun. Daytime temperatures reach as high as 840 degrees Fahrenheit (449°C). It is called "The Planetary Oven." At night, surface temps drop to -279°F (-173°C).

X**treme Fact**

NASA launched the MESSENGER spacecraft in 2004. Its main mission is to enter Mercury's orbit and study the planet.

# MERCURY

Mercury has little atmosphere. Meteors and comets often hit its surface, leaving it covered in craters.

# PLANET

Venus is named after the Roman goddess of beauty. On Earth, it appears brightly at sunrise or sunset. It is nicknamed "The Morning Star" and "The Evening Star." However, a close-up view shows that Venus is a hot world of volcanoes and lava flows. The toxic atmosphere is so dense that its surface pressure is 90 times greater than Earth's.

# VENUS

| Fahrenheit | Celsius | | |
|---|---|---|---|
| 1000° | 500° | | |
| 900° | | 🔵 | Venus |
| 800° | 400° | ⚫ | Mercury |
| 700° | | | |
| 200° | 100° | | |
| 100° | | 🌍 | Earth |
| 0° | 0° | ⚫ | Mars |
| -100° | -100° | 🪐 | Jupiter |
| -200° | | 🪐 | Saturn |
| -300° | -200° | 🔵 | Uranus |
| -400° | | 🔵 | Neptune |
| | | ⚫ | Pluto |

Planets not shown to scale.

**Xtreme Fact** Venus has the hottest temperature of any planet in our solar system.

# PLANET

Earth is unique in the solar system. It is the only known planet with liquid water. Its surface is about 70 percent water and 30 percent land. The water, along with Earth's distance from the Sun, keeps temperatures from becoming too hot or too cold. Earth's atmosphere helps protect the planet from small objects hurtling through space.

Arizona's Barringer Meteor Crater is 1 mile (1.6 km) wide and 570 feet (174 m) deep. This kind of impact is rare thanks to Earth's atmosphere protecting the planet.

# EARTH

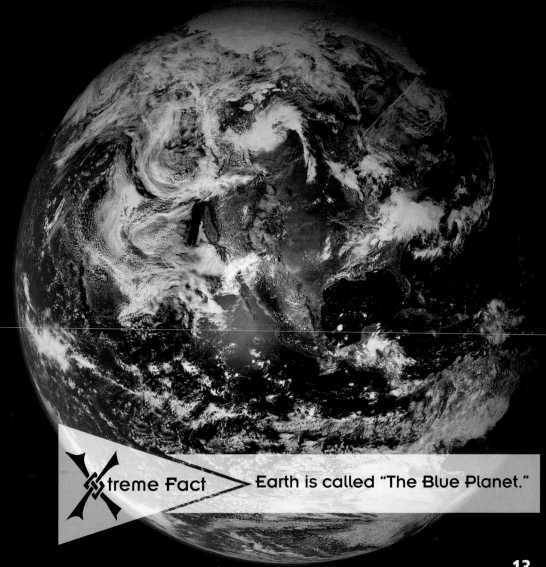

The *Galileo* spacecraft took these shots of the Earth and Moon, which were then combined into one image.

# Earth's Moon

The Moon is about 238,855 miles (384,400 km) from Earth. The Moon's diameter is 2,159 miles (3,475 km), about one-quarter that of Earth. It has deep craters, high hills, and even caves. However, it has no atmosphere, and no life has ever been found on Earth's nearest neighbor.

Xtreme Fact

The Sun is 400 times the Moon's diameter and about 400 times as far away from Earth. This makes the Sun and Moon look about the same size when viewed from Earth.

# PLANET

About half the size of Earth, Mars is called "The Red Planet." Mars is red because it is covered in a thin layer of dirt that is filled with rusty red iron clay. It is a cold, desert-like planet. Two moons orbit Mars.

Mars's moons

Deimos    Phobos

# MARS

NASA's Sojourner rover landed on Mars on July 4, 1997. It sent information and pictures for nearly three months. Several other NASA probes have since explored Mars.

# ASTEROID

# BELT

Asteroids are small, airless, rocky worlds that usually orbit our Sun. Each can be a few feet wide to several hundred miles wide. Thousands of asteroids have collected between the orbits of Mars and Jupiter. This is known as "The Asteroid Belt."

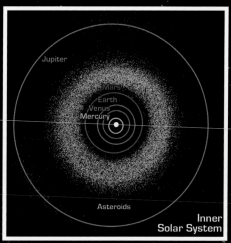

Jupiter

Mars
Earth
Venus
Mercury

Asteroids

Inner
Solar System

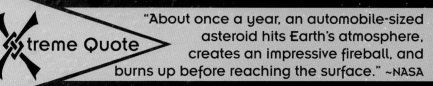

Xtreme Quote

"About once a year, an automobile-sized asteroid hits Earth's atmosphere, creates an impressive fireball, and burns up before reaching the surface." ~NASA

# PLANET

A photo of Jupiter's Great Red Spot.

Jupiter is called "The Giant Planet." It is the biggest planet in our solar system. More than 1,300 Earths would fit inside Jupiter. Jupiter's well-known feature, the Great Red Spot, is actually a huge storm that has raged for hundreds of years. Jupiter has 63 confirmed moons, the most of any planet.

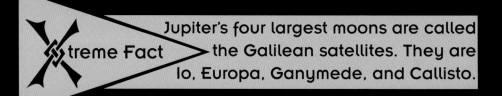

Xtreme Fact
Jupiter's four largest moons are called the Galilean satellites. They are Io, Europa, Ganymede, and Callisto.

# JUPITER

Jupiter is a gas giant. It does not have a solid surface like the Earth. Jupiter has so many moons, it is like a mini solar system.

Io is the closest moon to Jupiter.

Europa is about the size of Earth's Moon.

Callisto is similar in size and look to the planet Mercury.

Ganymede is the largest moon in the solar system.

# PLANET

Saturn is easily recognized for its unusual rings. Billions of chunks of ice and rock make up the rings. Many of them are believed to be pieces of comets, asteroids, and moons.

# SATURN

Like Jupiter, Saturn is a gas giant. Circling Saturn are at least 60 moons. Its biggest moon, Titan, is bigger than the planet Mercury.

# PLANET

Uranus is the seventh planet from the Sun. It was discovered in 1781 by astronomer William Herschel. Uranus is a gas giant. It is made up of gases, including methane. This gives the planet a blue-green glow.

Uranus has 27 known moons. New moons continue to be found as scientists study this distant planet.

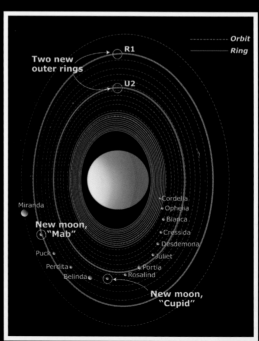

---------- Orbit
—————— Ring

R1

Two new outer rings

U2

Miranda

New moon, "Mab"

Puck

Perdita

Belinda

Cordelia
Ophelia
Bianca
Cressida
Desdemona
Juliet
Portia
Rosalind

New moon, "Cupid"

# URANUS

## Xtreme Fact

Uranus is not upright. It is tipped on its side. Scientists guess this happened when an object in space hit the planet.

# PLANET

Neptune is a cold, dark planet. It is 2.8 billion miles (4.5 billion km) from the Sun. It takes 165 Earth years for it to orbit the Sun. Neptune does not have a solid surface like Earth. The gas giant is covered in layers of thick clouds that blast across the planet at speeds up to 1,200 miles per hour (1,931 kph).

Triton

Xtreme Fact

Neptune has 13 known moons. The largest is called Triton.

# NEPTUNE

Neptune's Great Dark Spot is a storm that forms, changes shape, disappears, and reappears in a different place.

# Dwarf

Dwarf planets orbit the Sun and are usually round in shape. They are not big enough to have the gravity power to sweep up or scatter objects around their orbit. They are not moons of other planets. Pluto was once called our ninth planet. It is now classified as a dwarf planet. There are currently four others: Ceres, Haumea, Makemake, and Eris.

| Ceres | Haumea | Makemake | Eris |

# PLANETS

**X**treme Fact

Some astronomers say there may be hundreds of undiscovered dwarf planets in our solar system.

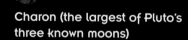

Charon (the largest of Pluto's three known moons)

Pluto

# THE

## Asteroid
A rocky or metal object that usually orbits the Sun.

## Diameter
The measurement of a straight line passing through an object from one side to the other.

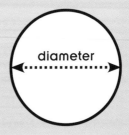

## Galilean Satellites
The four moons of Jupiter that the early Italian astronomer Galileo Galilei (1564-1642) was able to see: Ganymede, Callisto, Europa, and Io.

## Gas Giant
A huge planet made mostly of gases. There are four gas giants in our solar system: Jupiter, Saturn, Uranus, and Neptune. These are also called Jovian

# GLOSSARY

planets, named after the planet Jupiter. Many other gas giants have been found circling other stars.

## Meteor
A streak of light in the sky that occurs when space dust or a meteoroid (a metallic or stony space object) enters the atmosphere and burns up. A meteorite is an object that crashes to the Earth's surface.

## Methane
A gas found in the atmospheres of gas giants, as well as other solid planets and a few moons.

## National Aeronautics and Space Administration (NASA)
A U.S. government agency started in 1958. NASA's goals include space exploration, as well as increasing people's understanding of Earth, our solar system, and the universe.

# INDEX